HEIDI HECKELBECK
and the Big Mix-Up

By Wanda Coven
Illustrated by Priscilla Burris

LITTLE SIMON

New York London Toronto Sydney New Delhi

LITTLE SIMON

An imprint of Simon & Schuster Children's Publishing Division
1230 Avenue of the Americas, New York, New York 10020
First Little Simon hardcover edition September 2016
Copyright © 2016 by Simon & Schuster, Inc.
Also available in a Little Simon paperback edition.
All rights reserved, including the right of reproduction in whole or in part in any form.
LITTLE SIMON is a registered trademark of Simon & Schuster, Inc., and associated colophon is a trademark of Simon & Schuster, Inc.
For information about special discounts for bulk purchases, please contact
Simon & Schuster Special Sales at 1-866-506-1949
or business@simonandschuster.com.
The Simon & Schuster Speakers Bureau can bring authors to your live event.
For more information or to book an event contact
the Simon & Schuster Speakers Bureau at 1-866-248-3049
or visit our website at www.simonspeakers.com.
Designed by Ciara Gay
Manufactured in the United States of America 0816 FFG
10 9 8 7 6 5 4 3 2 1
Library of Congress Cataloging-in-Publication Data
Names: Coven, Wanda, author. | Burris, Priscilla, illustrator.
Title: Heidi Heckelbeck and the big mix-up / by Wanda Coven ; illustrated by Priscilla Burris. Description: First Little Simon hardcover/paperback edition. | New York : Little Simon, 2016. | Series: Heidi Heckelbeck ; 18 | Summary: An embarrassing rumor about Lucy spreads at school and she thinks Bruce is behind it so Heidi gets involved and uses some magic to bring the trio of friends back together. Identifiers: LCCN 2015047703| ISBN 9781481471701 (hardback) | ISBN 9781481471695 (paperback) | ISBN 9781481471718 (eBook) Subjects: | CYAC: Friendship—Fiction. | Witches—Fiction. | Rumor—Fiction. | Magic—Fiction. | Schools—Fiction. | BISAC: JUVENILE FICTION / Readers / Chapter Books. | JUVENILE FICTION / Fantasy & Magic. | JUVENILE FICTION / Imagination & Play. Classification: LCC PZ7.C83393 Hal 2016 | DDC [Fic]—dc23 LC record available at http://lccn.loc.gov/2015047703

CONTENTS

Chapter 1

SWEATER WEATHER

Flit!

Fly!

Flutter!

Fall leaves swirled and ticked the panes of Heidi's window. She pulled the hem of her quilt up to her chin. *I love fall!* she said to herself happily.

Then she remembered something else she loved: sweater weather! And the best part was, Heidi had a brand-new sweater.

She hopped out of bed and slipped on her fuzzy bunny slippers. Then she shuffled to her dresser and opened the bottom drawer. There it was—her new light-gray sweater. It had pink buttons up the front and pink stripes down the sleeves. On the lower right-hand side, sat an embroidered brown mouse in a white teacup. Heidi had gotten the sweater at Miss Harriet's store.

And now I finally get to wear it! she thought. She pulled on a jean skirt and a yellow tank top. Then she snuggled into her new sweater. She posed this way and that in front of the mirror. "Oh, it's SO cute!" she declared. Then she skipped downstairs to breakfast.

"Mmm," she murmured as she stepped into the kitchen. "What smells so good?"

Henry tapped the side of his head with his finger. "Hmm, let me think," he said. "Probably not YOU!"

Heidi rolled her eyes.

"It's cinnamon-apple oatmeal," said Dad, stirring a pan on the stove. He

had on Mom's red-checked apron.

Heidi held an empty bowl in front of Dad. "Fill it up, please!" she said.

Dad spooned steaming oatmeal into her bowl. Heidi lifted the bowl to her nose and breathed in the delicious scent.

"It smells like fresh apple pie," she said dreamily as she sat at the table.

"It tastes like it too," said Henry, licking his lips.

Mom glanced at Heidi. "Be careful not to get oatmeal on your new sweater," she said. "Henry already spilled some on his hoodie."

Heidi frowned at her brother. "Way to go, little bro," she said.

Henry shrugged. "Sometimes my clothes get hungry," he said. "Maybe that little mousie on your sweater wants some oatmeal too!"

"Not if I can help it," Heidi said as she placed a napkin on her lap.

Mom gave her a wink and a smile. "By the way, Heidi, I heard from Mrs. Welli that you have a publishing party at school on Friday. Parents are invited to hear students read their stories."

"Sounds like fun!" said Dad as he joined the family at the table. "Do you know what you're going to write about?"

Heidi blew on a spoonful of oatmeal. "Not yet," she said. "But I want it to be something special."

Then she took a big bite and gave her dad a thumbs-up. "I wonder if it would be too mushy to write about this oatmeal . . . because it's super-yummers!"

Chapter 2

T·W·i·N·S·i·E·S

Hippity!

Hoppity!

Bippity!

Boppity!

Heidi pranced down the hall-way toward her classroom. *My new sweater makes me SO happy,* she said to herself. *Or should I say "HOPPY"?* Then she waved to Lucy Lancaster and Bruce Bickerson at the other end of the hall. They waited for Heidi in front of the bulletin board.

Heidi took two steps back when she saw Lucy.

"No way! We have on the SAME sweater!" Heidi cried.

Lucy squealed and cupped her hand over her mouth.

"Well, it's a good thing I didn't wear mine," said Bruce with a smile.

Then the three friends burst into laughter.

Melanie Maplethorpe, Heidi's least favorite girl in the class, caught sight of the matching sweaters. She blinked very dramatically.

"Wow, am I seeing DOUBLE?" she asked.

Lucy leaned with her elbow on Heidi's shoulder. "What you're  seeing is double-good taste in clothes!" she said proudly.

Melanie's jaw dropped. "Did you actually PLAN those matchy-matchy outfits?" she said, pretending to be horrified.

"As a matter of fact, they DIDN'T," said Bruce, defending his friends.

"They were both TOTALLY surprised."

Melanie didn't like to be told what was what, so she tilted her head toward Bruce. "And how would YOU know?" she said, glaring at him. "Do you really think Heidi and Lucy would let YOU be part of their twinsy plan?"

Bruce swallowed uncomfortably.

Then Heidi and Lucy noticed and came to his rescue.

"Oh, don't listen to her, Bruce!" said Heidi.

"She doesn't know what she's talking about!" Lucy added.

Melanie shrugged. "Believe what you want, Bruce," she said with a sly smile. Then Melanie flipped her hair, twirled, and walked away.

Chapter 3

HURT FEELINGS

Br-r-r-r-r-ing!

The last bell of the day rang. The children thundered down the front steps of the school and lined up for either the bus line or the pickup line.

"Heidi! Lucy! Wait up!" shouted Bruce, who had gotten stuck behind a bunch of slow first graders.

The girls waited for Bruce by the playground.

"Wanna come over to my house this afternoon?" he asked breathlessly.

Heidi slung her backpack over her shoulder. "Sounds fun," she said. "But we already have plans."

Bruce's face fell. "What are you guys up to?" he asked.

"We're just going shopping," said Lucy, trying not to make it seem like a big deal.

Bruce bit his lower lip. "Do you have room for one more?" he asked hopefully.

Heidi nudged Lucy with the tip of her shoe.

"Um, well . . . ," Lucy began. She looked to Heidi for help.

Heidi shifted her feet. "Er, it's just that there's not enough room in Lucy's car," she said weakly.

Bruce raised an eyebrow. "Okay, what's going on with you two?" he asked.

Heidi made her eyes look big and round. "NOTHING'S going on!" she said a little too dramatically. "Right, Lucy?"

Lucy nodded swiftly in agreement.

"Absolutely nothing!" she said in a way that meant absolutely *something*.

Mrs. Lancaster pulled up in her silver minivan. The girls rushed to the door and hopped in. Bruce couldn't help but notice that there were still empty seats in the back.

"See you later, Bruce!" called Heidi as she closed the door and clicked

on her seat belt. As they rolled away she turned to Lucy. "Wow, that was close."

"You are NOT kidding!" Lucy agreed. "We can't let Bruce find out about our secret mission."

The girls took a deep breath and then giggled with excitement.

Chapter 4

GOSSiP GiRL

The next day, Lucy and Heidi waited for Bruce before class.

"I wish we could tell Bruce about our surprise," said Heidi. "I hate keeping secrets."

"Me too," said Lucy. "But the shop owner said our surprise would take

at least a few days."

Heidi slumped her shoulders. "I know. It's pure TORTURE," she said.

Lucy laughed. Then she checked her ladybug watch. "I wonder what's taking Bruce so long?"

Heidi shrugged. "Who knows? But here comes Laurel."

Laurel Lambert hurried up to the girls. Her eyes were wide and she looked worried.

"What's the matter?" asked Heidi.

Laurel looked over her shoulder

and then back at the girls. "Is it true what everyone's saying?" she asked.

The girls froze.

"About what?" asked Lucy.

"About YOU!" Laurel whispered.

Lucy pointed to herself. "ME?" she questioned.

Laurel nodded and whispered, "Everyone says you have LICE!"

As soon as Laurel said the word "lice," the kids in the hall scattered.

"Ewww!" cried Heidi. "That is so disgusting! Why would anyone ever say THAT?"

Lucy sniffled and fought back tears. "I . . . I don't know, but it's NOT true," she said, wiping the corner of her eye. "I don't have lice. Where did you hear that?"

Laurel clutched the straps of her backpack. "Everyone's been talking about it this morning," she said. Then she hung her head slightly. "I didn't think it was true, Lucy, but I thought you should know there's a rumor going around."

Heidi folded her arms tightly. "Who would start a horrible rumor about Lucy?" she said angrily. "Especially one as awful as LICE!"

"*Shhh,*" shushed Lucy. "Here comes Bruce."

Bruce was walking down the hall with Melanie and Stanley Stonewrecker. They walked right by the girls without even saying hello. Laurel followed them into the classroom.

"What was THAT all about?" questioned Heidi.

Lucy covered her face with her
hands and began to cry.

Heidi patted her friend on the back.

"Please don't cry," she begged. "We'll get to the bottom of this mystery."

"I'm sorry," wailed Lucy. "I have to go." Then she ran down the hall and disappeared into the nurse's office.

MR. SMARTY-PANTS

Rumors of lice rustled around the classroom all morning. Everyone had a case of the creepy crawlies. Some kids even began to scratch their heads. Heidi did her best to stick up for Lucy.

"It's all LIES!" she declared to anyone who would listen. Mrs. Welli tried

to reassure the children too, but it was no use. The whispering kept going all through math.

Heidi could not concentrate on her multiplication worksheet. She read the directions again: *Find the missing factor.* But it seemed like the only missing factor was Lucy. Heidi let out a great sigh. *I wonder if she'll come back to class?* Heidi checked the door every few minutes, but there was no sign of her friend.

At lunchtime, Heidi grabbed her lunch box and zoomed to the nurse's office.

"Is Lucy here?" asked Heidi.

Mrs. Foster, the school nurse, smiled. "Lucy went to the library a little while ago," she said.

"Did you have to check her head for

lice?" Heidi asked.

Mrs. Foster nodded
with understanding.
"Yes," she said. "And
Lucy is perfectly
fine."

Heidi whistled a sigh of relief. Then she went to the library.

Mrs. Williams, the librarian, was arranging papier-mâché ducks along the front of her desk.

"Make way for ducklings!" she said, and chuckled. Then she noticed Heidi's serious face. "Is there something I can do for you?" she asked.

Heidi looked around the library. "Have you seen Lucy Lancaster?" she asked hopefully.

Then Mrs. Williams pointed over to the Magic Tree Fort. "She's up there," whispered the librarian.

In the back of the library stood

a real tree house. It had a trunk, branches, leaves, and a ladder. The inside of the tree house had bean-bag chairs and mushroom pillows to hang out on and read books.

Heidi climbed the ladder and peered into the tree house. She saw Lucy lying on a yellow beanbag chair, looking at a book.

"Hey," Heidi began, setting down her lunch box. "I just wanted you to know, I told everybody the lice rumor wasn't true."

Lucy sighed and closed her book. "The only problem is that it WAS true," she said. "It happened a long time ago, before you started here. I don't have them anymore."

Heidi plopped onto a red polka-dot mushroom pillow next to Lucy.

"And I only told one person," Lucy
said.

"Who?" Heidi asked.

"BRUCE."

Heidi's eyes widened as she touched
Lucy's shoulder. "But why would Bruce
ever start a rumor about you?"

Lucy's face became furious. "I don't know," she said angrily. "But I know how to get back at him."

Heidi gulped. "How?" she asked.

Lucy sat up and looked at Heidi. "I'm going to tell everyone Bruce's SECRET!"

Heidi bit her thumbnail. "Bruce has a secret?"

Lucy nodded. "Did you know he almost changed

schools this year so he could be in an ADVANCED class?"

Heidi almost fell off her mushroom.

"That's because he thinks he's SMARTER than everyone else!" Lucy added.

Heidi had no idea that Bruce had been thinking about switching schools.

"We'll see how Mr. Smarty-Pants feels when the whole school finds out he thinks he's better than everyone!" said Lucy. Then she got up from her beanbag chair and began to climb down the ladder.

Heidi reached for Lucy's arm.

"Please don't say anything bad about Bruce," she said. "It won't help you feel better. In fact, it might make matters worse!"

Lucy had already made up her mind. She jumped off the bottom rung of the ladder and walked quickly out of the library.

Heidi picked up her lunch box. "Well, I have officially lost my appetite," she moaned.

MONKEY iN THE MiDDLE

Heidi clumped into the kitchen.

"How was your day?" asked Mom.

"Awful," said Heidi. "Lucy and Bruce are mad at each other."

Mom frowned. "That's too bad," she said. "I have something that might cheer you up." She placed a warm

ginger molasses
cookie and a
glass of milk on
the table.

Heidi sat down. "Where's Henry?"
she asked, sinking her teeth into the
soft, chewy cookie.

"At a friend's," said Mom.

"May I have his
cookie too?" asked
Heidi. "It's been a two-
cookie kind of day."

Just then the telephone rang.

"Of course, sweetie," Mom said,
and she answered the phone. "Hello?"

She listened and then covered the receiver. "It's Bruce," she whispered.

Heidi took a sip of milk and reached for the phone. Then she dragged a chair down the hall and into the closet for privacy.

"Hey, Bruce," Heidi said. "Are things better with Lucy?"

"Uh, no," said Bruce. "She told everyone that I think I'm the next EINSTEIN! Why would she DO that?"

Heidi felt terrible for both Bruce *and* Lucy.

"Well, um, maybe you shouldn't have started that lice rumor about Lucy," Heidi offered.

Bruce wasn't listening though. He just went on and on about what Lucy had done. Heidi had to hold the phone away from her ear.

Heidi heard the doorbell ring. Mom answered the door. Heidi peeked out from behind the closet door. *Oh my gosh, it's Lucy!* she said to herself. Heidi opened the door very quietly and waved to Lucy.

"Heidi!" Lucy cried. "I need to talk to you!"

Heidi leaned out of the closet door some more

and pointed toward the phone.

"Who are you talking to?" Lucy demanded.

Heidi covered the receiver. "Bruce!"

Lucy squinted her eyes. "Ugh, I am so mad at him right now! He's made my life miserable!"

Heidi put a finger to her lips. "He'll hear you!" she whispered.

"And why should I CARE?" said Lucy.

Heidi put the phone back up to her ear. "Is LUCY at your house?" Bruce asked.

"Um, she is," said Heidi meekly.

"What's SHE doing there?" he cried.

Then Lucy stamped her foot. "I cannot believe you're on the phone with BRUCE!" she complained.

Suddenly, Heidi felt like a monkey in the middle. Before Heidi could say anything, Bruce hung up, and Lucy stormed out the front door.

"What was THAT all about?" asked Mom, who came in to see what was going on.

Heidi handed Mom the phone.

"I'll tell you later," said Heidi. Then she ran out the front door to catch Lucy, but she was too late. Lucy was

gone. Heidi slumped down on her steps and cupped her chin in her hands.

Merg! It's like my friends are under a curse, she thought.

Chapter 7

SWEET TALK

Then Heidi had an idea. She jumped up and declared, "There's only one way to reverse a curse, and I know how to help!" Heidi ran straight to her room and pulled out her *Book of Spells* from under the bed. She found a spell called the Kindness Charm.

The Kindness Charm

Are you mad at your best friend? Or perhaps your best friend has become angry with you? Or worse yet, what if your two best friends are mad at each other? If you or your friends are fighting, then this is the spell for you!*

Ingredients:

4 candy conversation hearts

1 wooden clothespin

3 tablespoons of strawberry jam

1 glob of glue

Stir the ingredients together in a mixing bowl. Hold your Witches of Westwick medallion over your heart. Chant the following spell:

FUZZY WUZZY WHEE!

FUZZY WUZZY WOO!

MAKE MY FRIENDSHIPS

WARM AND FUZZY TOO!

* Charm only lasts one day, but one good day can help you find the best kind of magic.

Heidi laid her book on the floor. This was the perfect spell to make Lucy and Bruce stop fighting and like each other again. Proud of herself, Heidi got up to gather the ingredients. She found a box of last year's conversation hearts in her desk drawer,

which were underneath last year's valentines. She dumped the candy hearts onto her desk and turned them all face up. Then she picked four perfect hearts for the spell:

LOVE YOU | MISS YOU | BE KIND | BEST FRIENDS

Next she plucked a clothespin from the clothesline. After that, she

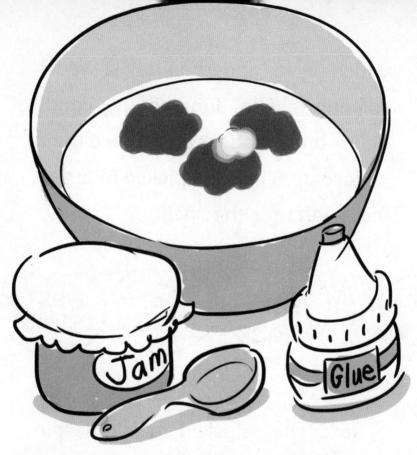

measured three tablespoons of strawberry jam and plopped them into a
mixing bowl. She followed this with
a glob of glue. Then she grabbed a

serving spoon and snuck back up to
her room.

Heidi dropped the candy hearts
into the mixing bowl
one at a time.
She added the
clothespin and
stirred the mix.

Then she slipped on her Witches of Westwick medallion and chanted the spell.

Whoosh! A rainbow cloud floated up from the bowl and sailed out the window.

"Happy friendships, here we come!" Heidi cheered.

Chapter 8

MISSING IN ACTION

Heidi tapped her pencil on her desktop and looked at the clock. *Where on earth are Lucy and Bruce?* she wondered. *They're never late for school!* Then Mrs. Welli called the class to attention.

"Good morning, boys and girls!"

she sang. "Let's begin by moving our desks around. You may sit next to whomever you'd like."

The students looked at one another in surprise. Mrs. Welli never let friends sit next to one another! It was too tempting to talk. Heidi wondered if this had something to do with the Kindness Charm. Then everyone began to move desks around.

Heidi pushed her desk next to Lucy's and Bruce's desks—even though they hadn't gotten to school yet. Laurel pushed her desk to the other side of Heidi's. Of course, Melanie banged

the edge of her desk next to Stanley's.

"Now, who would like to change up our lesson order today, too, so that we can work on our thankful project first?" asked Mrs. Welli.

"ME!" shouted the entire class.

"Good!" said their teacher. Then she passed out orange, yellow, and red construction paper.

Mrs. Welli had the class make hand-y thank-you wreath decorations. She showed everyone how to trace a hand on the construction paper. They

each traced twelve hands in all. Then
they cut them out. The hands became
the leaves. They arranged the leaves in
the shape of a wreath and glued them
together. On each leaf, they wrote
something to be thankful for.

"This is way better than starting the day with math," said Laurel.

Heidi agreed.

Melanie stopped in front of Heidi's desk on her way to the pencil sharpener. She smiled sweetly. "That's a

cute owl top you have on," she said.

Heidi looked at her shirt and then back at Melanie.

"Thanks!" said Heidi. Had Melanie just given her a compliment? Now Heidi was sure that it was the

Kindness Charm talking. Still, it was a nice change. Then she wrote, *I'm thankful for kind words* on one of her leaves.

Laurel tapped Heidi on the shoulder. "Do you know where Lucy and Bruce are today?" she asked.

Heidi shook her head. "I've been wonder- ing the same thing." She raised her hand and asked Mrs. Welli.

I'm thankful for kind words.

Her teacher went and reviewed the attendance sheet. "It looks like both Lucy and Bruce called out absent today," she said. "I hope they're feeling all right."

"I hope so too," Heidi said as she started a second thank-you wreath. *Oh darn,* thought Heidi. *Lucy and*

Bruce have to be near each other in order for the Kindness Charm to work on them.

The charm seemed to be working in full force on everyone else. Melanie gave Heidi a red licorice rope at lunch. Principal Pennypacker

declared it More Recess Day and gave
Heidi's class three recesses. And then
Mrs. Williams gave all her students

hedgehog erasers. Kindness was in full bloom for everyone at Brewster Elementary—everyone except Lucy and Bruce.

Heidi sighed. She knew that this charm only lasted for a single day. It was time to come up with a new plan.

Chapter 9

ONE GOOD STORY

On Friday, the Kindness Spell had worn off completely. Melanie insulted Heidi's outfit. Mrs. Welli made everyone move their desks back to their original places. And Lucy and Bruce had returned to school, but they still weren't talking. *Well, at least we're having the publishing party today,* Heidi thought. She had worked on her story until way past bedtime.

The children unfolded chairs and

set them in rows for the party. They also hung a banner with quotes from their favorite children's books. Heidi chose "Let the wild rumpus start!"

The class also laid out snacks on a party table. Melanie's mother had brought homemade sugar cookies in the shape of open books.

Near the end of the day the parents filled all the chairs. Heidi opened her folder to the story she had written. She couldn't wait to share it.

Mrs. Welli greeted the parents and thanked them for coming. She told them how hard the children had worked on their stories.

"Who would like to share first?" the teacher asked.

Heidi's hand shot up, and her teacher called on her. Heidi picked

up her notebook paper and stood beside her desk. She nodded to Mrs. Welli and began to read.

"'Best Friends,' by Heidi Heckelbeck. Have you ever been the new kid at school?" Heidi began as she looked at the audience. Most of the parents

smiled and nodded with understanding.

"Well, I have," she went on, "and it's pretty scary. When I started second grade at Brewster Elementary, I didn't know ANYBODY in my whole class. I felt like an ALIEN. Then the girl who sat two rows away turned around and smiled. Her smile made me feel a teensy-weensy bit better.

"At lunch I sat at a table all by myself. I felt so uncomfortable. Then something wonderful happened. That same girl who had smiled at me in class asked if she could sit next to me. I said, 'Yes, of course!' Lucy and I have been great friends ever since."

Heidi stopped reading and smiled at Lucy. Lucy smiled back.

"On the second day of school," Heidi went on, "I had to take the bus for the first time. I sat next to Lucy's friend Bruce. Then something crazy happened. The school bully, who was sitting in the seat behind us, bonked Bruce on the head with his backpack! Bruce's glasses went flying! I quickly dropped to my knees and found his glasses on the floor. I also found the bully's feet, so I untied his shoelaces. This made the bully trip when he got off the bus."

Heidi's classmates and the parents all laughed.

"Bruce and I laughed our heads off too," Heidi continued. "We have been great friends from that day on.

"Now the three of us do everything together. We make leaf piles and

jump in them. We do school projects and play games together. Once in a while, but not very often, we have a misunderstanding—like the time when Lucy got a sparkly light-up lollipop pen. I loved her pen SO much, and I wanted one just like it! Then one day the lollipop pen went missing. To make matters way worse, Lucy

thought I was the THIEF! That hurt my feelings.

"When Lucy's pen still hadn't turned up, I felt terrible. That afternoon Bruce and I played a game of Frisbee in his backyard. His dog,

Frankie, kept stealing the Frisbee! Then Frankie ran off with the Frisbee and hid it inside his doghouse. Bruce had to crawl into the doghouse to get it. Do you know what else he found in there?" asked Heidi, looking up.

"Lucy's lollipop pen! The dog had been the thief all along.

"What I'm trying to say is that sometimes friends get mad at each other. Sometimes they get so mad, they won't even talk about why they are mad, and they can't remember why they like each other. And that's why I wrote this story, because I love my two best friends. They make me smile and laugh every day. My friend Lucy is so nice, and Bruce is the smartest, most inventive person I know. I hope we can stay best friends forever."

Heidi glanced at the audience and walked back to her desk. Then everyone clapped and cheered.

Chapter 10

NO SURPRISE

Heidi grabbed a sugar cookie from the party table and took a huge bite. *Yum!* she thought. *Nothing like a good book!* Then Lucy and Bruce ran up to Heidi and wrapped their arms around her.

"Group hug!" Lucy declared. Heidi

dropped her cookie and squeezed her two friends happily.

"Heidi, your story was the BEST," Lucy said.

"And we both needed to hear it," added Bruce.

Lucy and Bruce looked at each other within the huddle.

"I'm so sorry I said those things about you, Bruce," said Lucy.

"No, I'M sorry!" Bruce insisted.

"No, really," said Lucy, "I am!"

Then Heidi pulled out of the hug.

"Will you two stop?" said Heidi. "It was all just a big mix-up." Then she handed her friends two paper plates. "Here, have some snacks!" she suggested.

The friends loaded their plates and sat down in the reading nook.

"I just have to admit one more thing, Lucy," said Bruce, lowering his eyes. "I really didn't mean to tell Melanie your secret. It just kind of slipped out. The truth is, I felt so left out when you  and Heidi went shopping without me the other day. Then Melanie told me it meant that maybe you guys didn't like me anymore."

Lucy and Heidi both dropped their cookies.

"Oh no!" exclaimed Lucy. "You've got it ALL wrong!"

Heidi nodded wildly. "The only reason we left you out was because we had a super-big surprise for you!"

Bruce stared at the girls in dis-
belief. "A surprise?" he said.

Lucy and Heidi both nodded at the
same time.

"Come on—let's go get my mom!"
said Lucy. "Then we can show you!"

Lucy, Bruce, and Heidi followed Mr. and Mrs. Lancaster to their mini-van. Mrs. Lancaster reached into the back of the van and pulled out a blue plastic bag. She handed it to Lucy.

"This is what we were up to," said Lucy. She pulled a T-shirt from the bag and held it up.

It read: BEST FRIENDS FOREVER across the front.

"We had one made for all three of us," Heidi added triumphantly.

Then the three friends put on their new T-shirts.

"We should've told you sooner," said Heidi, "but we wanted it to be a surprise."

Bruce laughed. "Well, it's NO surprise to me because we are definitely best friends forever."

Then they all bumped fists and burst out laughing. Heidi was so happy to have Lucy and Bruce back because friends truly are the best kind of magic.

Check out the next book starring

Sporty cardboard signs dangled from the gym ceiling. Each one had something written on it in fat, colorful letters: RUN!, JUMP!, KICK!, and BATTER UP! There was even a banner on the wall behind the bleachers that said GET MOVING! Tables with ruffled skirts stood all around the gym. Each table had a

An excerpt from *Heidi Heckelbeck Tries Out for the Team*

Check out the next book starring

Sporty cardboard signs dangled from the gym ceiling. Each one had something written on it in fat, colorful letters: RUN!, JUMP!, KICK!, and BATTER UP! There was even a banner on the wall behind the bleachers that said GET MOVING! Tables with ruffled skirts stood all around the gym. Each table had a

An excerpt from Heidi Heckelbeck Tries Out for the Team

poster with a different sport on it: SOCCER, BASEBALL, VOLLEYBALL, BASKETBALL, TRACK AND FIELD, and CHEERLEADING.

"What's up with all the sports stuff?" Heidi asked.

Lucy Lancaster shrugged and nudged Bruce Bickerson. "Do you know?"

"Looks like a sports fair," Bruce said as they climbed the bleachers and sat with the rest of the students.

Principal Pennypacker stood in front of the school with a micro-phone. "Good morning, Brewster sports fans!" he said as he smoothed

An excerpt from *Heidi Heckelbeck Tries Out for the Team*

one of the tufts of hair on the side of his head.

"Good morning!" the students responded.

The principal motioned toward the tables. "Who likes sports?" he asked.

The students clapped and hooted their approval. Everyone except Heidi. She didn't dislike sports, but they had never really been her thing. She waited to hear more.

"Today we kick off our new after-school sports program," he explained. "Everyone gets to pick a sport and try it out."

An excerpt from *Heidi Heckelbeck Tries Out for the Team*